Way Up High
in a
Tall Green Tree

by
Jan Peck

illustrated by
Valeria Petrone

SIMON & SCHUSTER BOOKS FOR YOUNG READERS
New York London Toronto Sydney

To Joanna Feliz, Kevin L. Lewis, Lucy Ruth Cummins, Katrina Groover, and Valeria Petrone:
My HIGHEST appreciation and admiration for all you've accomplished! –J. P.

SIMON & SCHUSTER BOOKS FOR YOUNG READERS
An imprint of Simon & Schuster Children's Publishing Division
1230 Avenue of the Americas, New York, New York 10020
Text copyright © 2005 by Jan Peck
Illustrations copyright © 2005 by Valeria Petrone
All rights reserved, including the right of reproduction in whole or in part in any form.
SIMON & SCHUSTER BOOKS FOR YOUNG READERS is a trademark of Simon & Schuster, Inc.
Book design by Lucy Ruth Cummins
The text for this book is set in Fink Heavy.
The illustrations for this book are rendered digitally.
Manufactured in China
6 8 10 9 7
Library of Congress Cataloging-in-Publication Data
Peck, Jan.
Way up high in a tall green tree / Jan Peck ; illustrated by Valeria Petrone.– 1st ed.
p. cm.
Summary: A girl climbs a tree in the rain forest saying good night to all the creatures,
but it is really her bunk bed as she settles down with all her stuffed animals.
ISBN 978-1-4169-0071-9 (alk. paper)
[1. Rain forest animals–Fiction. 2. Animals–Fiction. 3. Bedtime–Fiction. 4. Stories in rhyme.] I. Petrone, Valeria, ill. II. Title.
PZ8.3.P2754Wb 2005   [E]–dc22   2004028408
0815 SCP

For my edifying editors, Kevin L. Lewis and Joanna Feliz,
my way up highest appreciation and love—J. P.

To Alice, Lorenzo, Flavia, and Marco—V. P.

Way up high in a tall green tree,
I'm climbing to the tippy-top
to see what I can see.
I'm so brave,
can't scare me,
way up high in a tall green tree.

Way up high in a tall green tree,
I spy an ocelot napping by me.
Hello, ocelot.
Lots of spots, ocelot.
See you later, ocelot.

Climb away.

Way up high in a tall green tree,
I spy a kinkajou swinging by me.
Hello, kinkajou.
Loop-de-loo, kinkajou?
See you later, kinkajou.

Climb away.

Way up high in a tall green tree,
I spy a sloth hokey-pokey by me.
Hello, hairy sloth.
S-l-o-w M-o, hairy sloth.
See you later, hairy sloth.

Climb away.

Way up high in a tall green tree,
I spy a boa who wants to hug me.
Hello, boa.
Squeeze please, boa.
See you later, boa.

Climb away.

Way up high in a tall green tree,
I spy a parrot chatting with me.
Hello, parrot.
Yakity-yak, parrot.
See you later, parrot.

Climb away.

Way up high in a tall green tree,
I spy a gecko hiding by me.
Hello, gecko.
Hide-n-seek, gecko.
See you later, gecko.

Climb away.

Way up high in a tall green tree,
I spy a bat topsy-turvy by me.
Hello, little bat.
Wake up, little bat.
See you later, little bat.

Climb away.

Way up high in a tall green tree,
I spy a tree frog winking at me.
Hello, tree frog.
Googly-eyed, tree frog.
See you later, tree frog.

Climb away.

Way up high in a tall green tree,
I spy a butterfly floating by me.
Hello, butterfly.
Touch the sky, butterfly.
See you later, butterfly.

Climb away.

Way up high in a tall green tree,
I spy the moon smiling down upon me!

Nighty-night, moon.

Nighty-night, butterfly.
Nighty-night, tree frog.
Nighty-night, little bat.
Nighty-night, gecko.

Nighty-night, parrot.
Nighty-night, boa.
Niiiiightyyyyy-niiiiight, haiiiiry sloth.
Nighty-night, kinkajou.
Nighty-night, ocelot.

Down, down, down from a tall green tree,
I find Daddy waiting for me.
Hello, Daddy!
Guess what, Daddy?
I climbed to the top of a tall green tree!